AF448160

Written by Chris Levine
Illustrations by Olesea Vladimir
Copyright, Scary Dinosaur Stories © 2023

jurassic terrors

HAUNTING STORIES OF DINOSAURS

Contents

The Aerial Assault

Carrie and Jack had always shared a love for adventure, which led them to embark on an exciting journey in their small Cessna airplane. They planned to fly across the country, taking in the breathtaking landscapes and visiting remote locations along the way.

As they set off on their aerial adventure, the skies were clear and the winds were calm. They soared above the beautiful countryside, marveling at the vast expanses of land that stretched out beneath them.

However, their carefree journey took a turn for the worse when they encountered an unexpected and violent storm. Powerful gusts of wind battered their tiny aircraft, forcing them to veer off course and struggle to maintain control.

As they fought to navigate through the storm, an eerie sight appeared before them. A group of pterodactyls, massive prehistoric flying reptiles, emerged from the dark clouds, their leathery wings beating the air as they swooped and circled around the Cessna.

Terrified and disoriented, Carrie and Jack tried to evade the aggressive creatures, performing evasive maneuvers in the hopes of shaking them off their tail. The pterodactyls, however, seemed determined to attack the small aircraft, their sharp beaks and claws causing damage to the plane's wings and fuselage.

With each passing moment, the situation grew more dire. Carrie and Jack knew that they needed to find a way to escape the relentless pursuit of the pterodactyls and safely navigate

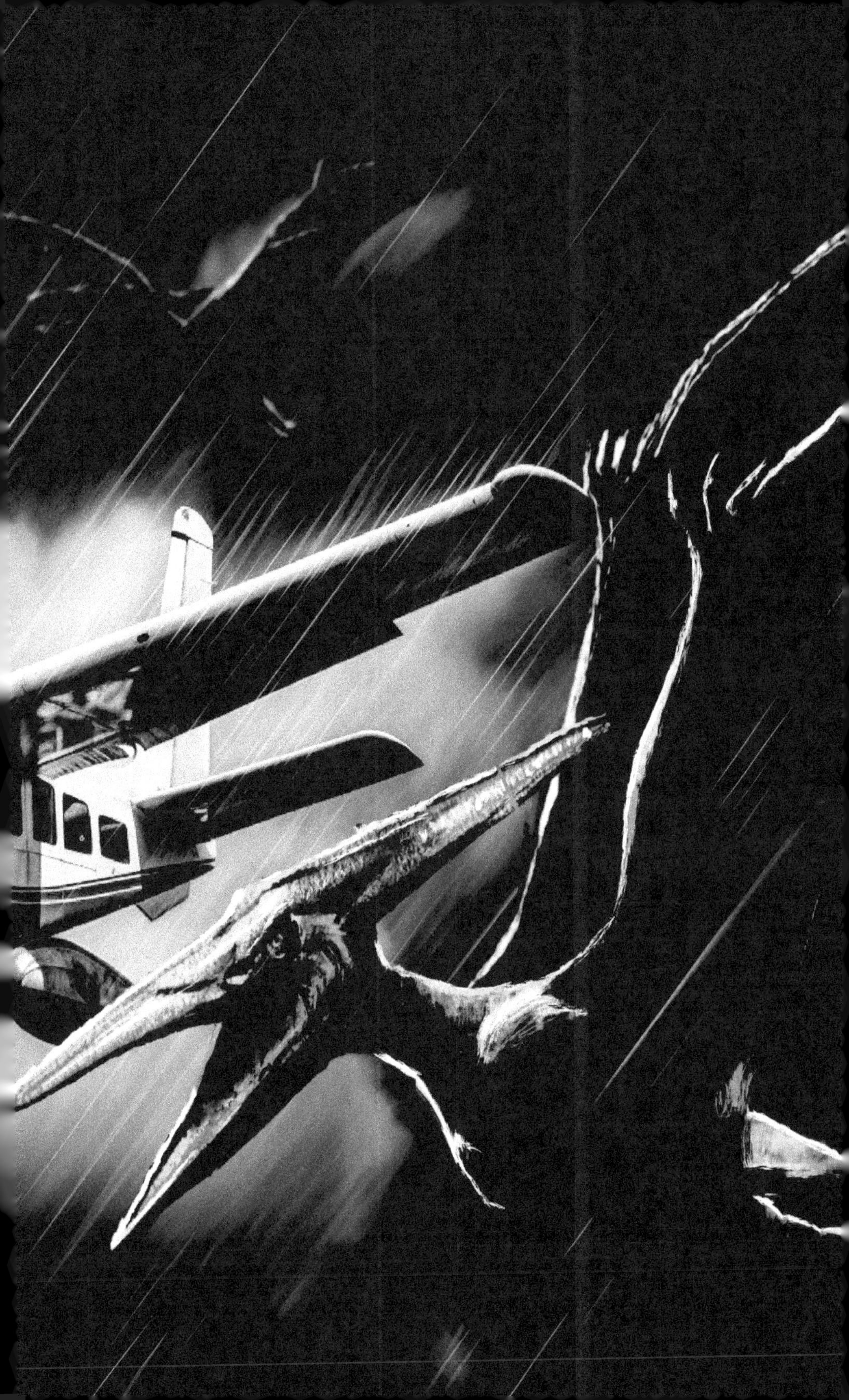

through the storm. Their minds raced, searching for a solution to their life-threatening predicament. As the pterodactyls continued to attack the small Cessna airplane, one of them managed to tear a piece of the wing, causing the aircraft to shake violently. Carrie and Jack's hearts pounded in their chests, their fear mounting with each terrifying swoop of the enormous creatures.

Thinking quickly, Jack remembered the flare gun stored in the emergency kit under his seat. He grabbed it and fired a bright red flare at the closest pterodactyl. The sudden burst of light and heat momentarily stunned the creature, causing it to veer off course and collide with another pursuing pterodactyl.

The sudden reprieve from their attackers allowed Carrie and Jack to focus on navigating through the storm. With rain lashing at the windscreen and lightning illuminating the dark sky, they struggled to maintain control of the plane.

Jack fought to keep the Cessna steady, pushing the throttle to gain altitude and escape the fury of the storm. Carrie, meanwhile, frantically scanned the cockpit for any tools or instruments that might help them evade the remaining pterodactyls.

Spotting a small fire extinguisher, Carrie had an idea. She opened the window, bracing herself against the howling wind, and aimed the extinguisher at the nearest pterodactyl. She pulled the trigger, releasing a powerful jet of foam that blinded the creature, sending it plummeting into the darkness below.

With the pterodactyls temporarily dealt with, Jack and Carrie focused all their energy on surviving the storm. They knew they couldn't outrun it forever, but they were determined to give it their all.

As they flew higher, they caught a glimpse of a small airstrip on the edge of a clearing. Jack, fueled by adrenaline, managed to navigate the damaged plane towards it, expertly dodging lightning strikes and powerful gusts of wind.

And as the storm began to subside and the pterodactyls retreated, Jack made an emergency landing on the tiny airstrip. Their hearts still racing from the harrowing ordeal, Carrie and Jack embraced, grateful to have survived the terrifying encounter with the prehistoric creatures.

Their harrowing encounter with the prehistoric creatures became a tale of survival and quick thinking in the face of seemingly insurmountable odds Carrie and Jack's story served as a reminder of the power of the natural world and the resilience of the human spirit when confronted with unimaginable dangers.

Despite the terrifying ordeal, the couple remained undeterred in their pursuit of adventure. They continued to explore the skies and share their love for flight, their hearts forever bound by the memories of their narrow escape from the jaws of the ancient predators that had once ruled the skies.

The Summer Camp Nightmare

David had always been the adventurous type, so when he received an urgent text message from his friends about a mysterious deserted summer camp, he couldn't resist the urge to investigate. They had gone there to explore the abandoned campgrounds, but their message hinted at something gone terribly wrong.

As David approached the eerie, overgrown camp, he felt a growing sense of unease. The once-vibrant playgrounds and cabins were now consumed by nature, their decaying structures casting long shadows in the fading light. The only sound was the rustling of leaves and the occasional snapping of twigs underfoot.

His heart pounding, David began to search the camp for any signs of his friends. As he delved deeper into the desolate area, he discovered something far more terrifying than he could have ever imagined: velociraptors, long thought to be extinct, roamed the campgrounds, hunting for prey.

Realizing the immense danger, David desperately searched for his friends, avoiding the raptors as best as he could. The campgrounds, once familiar and comforting, had transformed into a treacherous maze teeming with lethal predators.

As he made his way through the winding paths and abandoned cabins, David stumbled upon a raptor feasting on an unfortunate victim, from what was left of him, it was Michelle, a friend of many years. He covered his mouth quickly to try to contain his sadness. But the creature heard him already, it lifted its blood-stained snout and locked eyes with David, letting out a chilling screech before lunging towards him. Thinking quickly,

David ran towards an open cabin and just as the raptor leaped
to attack he dove to his left causing the beast to fly right into
the cabin, David quickly stood and shut the cabin door narrowly avoiding the raptor's snapping jaws and locking it inside.

Moving towards the main building David found himself cornered in the camp's dining hall. As a raptor stalked closer, its
talons clicking ominously against the floor, he spotted a fire
extinguisher on the wall. With no other option, he grabbed the
canister and sprayed its contents directly at the raptor's face,
buying himself precious seconds to escape through a nearby
window.

Continuing his frantic search, David heard distant cries for
help. Following the sound, he came across his other two
friends, Sarah and Kevin, trapped on the roof of a cabin as
raptors circled below. Using a nearby rope, David climbed
the closest tree and threw the rope onto the roof. They tied
it to the chimney top and as quietly as they could grappled
across the makeshift zipline to the tree. They hugged each
other with tears of joy as David whispered to them that he saw
a boathouse and maybe they could use that to get away. They
nodded and each one of them carefully climbed down the tree
all while the pack of raptors still circled the cabin hoping for
another meal.

The smell of gasoline and damp wood filled the air, as they
cautiously made their way through the dimly lit boathouse,
stepping over discarded oars and fishing equipment.

Suddenly, the silence was shattered by a raptor's guttural growl
echoing through the boathouse. Sarah yelped out of shock
as Kevin covered her mouth. The creature's shadow slowly
creeping along the wall. They knew they had to think fast to
escape the impending danger.

Spotting a small rowboat hanging from the ceiling, David quickly climbed onto it, hoping the raptor wouldn't notice him in the darkness. The raptor entered the boathouse, sniffing the air and scanning the room with its predatory gaze.

As the raptor neared the rowboat, David's heart raced. He knew he needed a distraction to divert the creature's attention. Glancing around, he noticed a tin of paint thinner on a nearby shelf. Desperate, he grabbed the can and threw it towards the far end of the boathouse. The tin clattered against the floor, its contents spilling and filling the air with a strong, pungent odor.

The raptor's attention immediately shifted to the source of the noise, giving David and his friends the opportunity he needed. He carefully lowered himself from the rowboat and together they slipped out of the boathouse, trying their best not to make a sound. The raptor, now thoroughly disoriented by the paint thinner fumes, struggled to regain its bearings, allowing them to make an escape.

Making a run for it, the group sprinted towards the camp's entrance, the sound of the raptors' footsteps growing louder with each passing moment.

As they raced through the decaying camp, a deafening roar echoed through the air, stopping them in their tracks. A massive Tyrannosaurus rex emerged from the woods, its menacing eyes fixed on the group. David and his friends knew they stood no chance against the colossal predator, but they had no choice but to keep running.

The chase led them to the edge of a steep cliff, with the T. rex gaining ground every second. Cornered and out of options, David and his friends braced themselves for the inevitable. Just as the dinosaur lunged towards them, a hail of arrows soared through the air, striking the T. rex and causing it to stagger back.

To their astonishment, a local tribe of Native Americans emerged from the surrounding forest, their bows and arrows aimed at the fearsome creature. Working together, they managed to distract the T. rex, providing David and his friends with a narrow window to escape.

With the help of the Native American tribe, the group managed to scale down the cliffside, putting a safe distance between themselves and the deadly predators. As they made their way to safety, the tribe explained that they had been protecting the area for generations, keeping the prehistoric creatures contained and out of sight from the rest of the world.

Relieved and grateful, David thanked the tribe for their bravery and selflessness. He and his friends knew they owed their lives to these courageous individuals, who had risked everything to save them from the terrifying beasts that had once ruled the Earth.

While the world remained largely unaware of the hidden dangers that lurked within the deserted summer camp, David and his friends would never forget the heroes who had saved them from the nightmare that had unfolded in the shadows of the ancient forest.

The Jungle's Wrath

The Thompson family had always been fond of adventure, seeking out new and exciting experiences to share together. So, when they decided to charter a plane for an unforgettable journey to a remote jungle, no one was surprised.

The lush, vibrant landscape of the jungle was the perfect setting for the Thompsons to explore and bond as a family. Excitedly, they prepared for the trip, ensuring they had all the necessary gear and provisions for their adventure.

As the small plane soared above the dense jungle canopy, the family gazed down in awe at the vast expanse of green that stretched out beneath them. They eagerly anticipated the unique wildlife and fascinating discoveries that awaited them in the untamed wilderness below.

However, their excitement was short-lived as a sudden, violent storm swept in, causing their plane to be tossed about by powerful gusts of wind. The pilot struggled to maintain control, but the fierce storm proved too much for the small aircraft.

With a gut-wrenching lurch, the plane plummeted towards the jungle floor, crashing through the thick canopy before coming to a screeching halt among the tangled undergrowth. The Thompsons found themselves battered and bruised but miraculously alive, their adventure taking a terrifying turn.

Their plane destroyed and the pilot dead they assessed their situation and took stock of their injuries, the family realized they were stranded in the heart of the jungle with no way to call for help. Determined to survive and find a way home, they set out to explore their surroundings in search of rescue.

Unbeknownst to them, a deadly predator was lurking in the shadows, drawn to the scent of the crashed plane and its human occupants. The Spinosaurus, a formidable and cunning carnivore, stalked the Thompsons as they moved through the dense foliage, its predatory instincts driving it to close in on its prey.

After what seemed like hours of traversing through the dense jungle the family decided to take a break and catch their breath. Tired and fearful they each began sniffing the pungent air around them. Confused on what would cause this bad of a smell until behind a nearby bush they found a partially eaten Jaguar, rotting and covered in flies.

Just then the ground beneath them began to tremble, and the air filled with a low, guttural growl. Paralyzed with fear, they watched in terror as a colossal Spinosaurus emerged from the foliage, its massive sail-like fin slicing through the air. The creature towered over the family, its razor-sharp teeth bared in a predatory snarl. The Spinosaurus lunged towards them, ready to snatch them in its powerful jaws, but the Thompsons made a split-second decision to dive inside of a fallen tree. The creature's teeth clashed together with a deafening crunch, just inches from where they had been standing moments before. Momentarily distracted by the carcass of the dead cat, it leaned down, nudged it and in one quick snap swallowed it whole. But it wasn't done. It sniffed the air. It knew the family was still around. It then looked at the tree. The tree the Thompsons were hiding in. It reared up on its hind legs and stormed towards the trunk smashing it to pieces but under its clawed foot there was nothing...

As the family trekked deeper into the jungle, still shaking from the carnivorous dinosaur they just encountered, they stumbled upon an old radio tower, long abandoned by its former occupants. Desperate for a way to call for help, they climbed the

rusted structure, hoping to find a functioning radio at its summit.

However, their attempt to reach safety was interrupted by the sudden reappearance of the Spinosaurus, its massive jaws and razor-sharp teeth poised to strike. The family scrambled up the tower with newfound urgency, narrowly avoiding the predator's snapping jaws as it lunged at them from below.

As the Spinosaurus continued to menace the terrified family, they discovered a still-functional radio in the tower's control room. With trembling fingers, they sent out a frantic distress call, praying that someone would hear them and come to their rescue.

After what felt like an eternity, a voice crackled through the radio, confirming that a rescue helicopter was on its way. The Thompsons, relieved and exhausted, huddled together in the control room, watching in terror as the Spinosaurus circled the base of the tower, waiting for them to descend.

Finally, the unmistakable sound of a helicopter's rotor blades filled the air, and the family watched as their rescuers appeared above the jungle canopy. As the helicopter lowered a rescue harness, the Spinosaurus roared in frustration, realizing that its prey was about to escape its grasp.

One by one, the Thompsons were hoisted into the helicopter, their hearts pounding with fear and relief as they left the Spinosaurus and the jungle behind. As they soared away from the scene of their harrowing ordeal, they knew that their lives had been forever changed by their brush with the jungle's wrath.

Depths of the Megalodon: The Sunken Treasure

Liam and Emma, two adventurous teens, had been looking forward to their vacation by the sea for months. Both avid scuba divers, they eagerly planned an underwater excursion to explore the mysterious depths of the ocean, hoping to discover hidden treasures and experience the beauty of marine life.

On the day of their dive, the weather was perfect, and the ocean's surface was calm and inviting. After gearing up and going through their safety checks, Liam and Emma plunged into the crystal-clear waters, eager to begin their aquatic adventure.

As they swam deeper into the ocean, they marveled at the vibrant colors of the coral reefs and the fascinating creatures that inhabited them. The two friends were in awe of the underwater world they were discovering, feeling a sense of freedom and wonder.

Their exploration took them to a location rumored to hold the wreckage of an ancient ship, the 'Esmeralda', which had sunk centuries ago, laden with gold and other precious treasures. Intrigued by the possibility of unearthing long-lost riches, Liam and Emma ventured further into the depths.

Suddenly, the tranquility of their dive was shattered when a massive shadow loomed above them. They could hardly believe their eyes as they realized they were face-to-face with a Megalodon shark, a monstrous prehistoric predator thought to be extinct. The creature's immense size and razor-sharp teeth struck fear into their hearts, as they knew they were no match for the powerful beast.

With adrenaline pumping through their veins, Liam and
Emma knew they had to act quickly to avoid becoming the
Megalodon's next meal. They swam towards an underwater
cave system, hoping that its twisting tunnels would provide
them with some form of protection and a chance to escape the
relentless predator.

As they navigated the narrow passageways of the caves, the
Megalodon's powerful tail thrashed in pursuit, stirring up
clouds of sand and sending smaller marine life fleeing in
terror. The two friends knew they couldn't keep evading the
massive shark forever and began to search for a way to fend off
their attacker.

In the depths of the caves, they stumbled upon the sunken
ship they had been seeking, the 'Esmeralda'. Its corroded hull
and tattered sails were a testament to the passage of time. Liam
and Emma decided to search the ship for anything that could
help them fend off the Megalodon.

As they delved into the wreckage, they discovered a cache of
old-fashioned harpoons, their rusted tips still sharp enough
to pierce the shark's thick skin. They also found a chest filled
with gold coins, glittering in the faint light that penetrated the
depths. Eager to claim the treasure, they quickly stuffed some
coins into their dive bags before preparing to face the Megalodon.

Armed with their newfound weapons, Liam and Emma prepared to make their stand against the Megalodon. As the shark
closed in, they steadied their nerves and swam out from the
shelter of the caves to face their fearsome foe.

The two teens took turns attacking the shark, one distracting
it while the other aimed for its sensitive gills and eyes. Despite
its size and power, the Megalodon began to falter, weakened

by the relentless onslaught. Sensing their opportunity, Liam and
Emma combined their efforts, driving their harpoons deep into
the creature's vulnerable spots.

The Megalodon, injured and disoriented, retreated into the
depths, leaving the two friends battered but alive. They knew
they had been extremely lucky and quickly made their way to
the surface, grateful for their narrow escape.

Exhausted but triumphant, Liam and Emma returned to shore,
the weight of the gold coins in their dive bags a constant reminder of the incredible adventure they had just experienced.
Word of their harrowing encounter with the Megalodon and
their discovery of the long-lost treasure spread like wildfire
among the locals and tourists alike. Soon, news outlets and marine biologists descended upon the coastal town, eager to hear
the teens' extraordinary story and learn more about the mysterious Megalodon.

The Desolation of Raptor's Hollow

On a dark and stormy night, a group of five friends, Mark, Jessica, Noah, Lily, and Chloe, were on their way home from a road trip when their car suddenly sputtered to a stop. Stranded in the middle of nowhere, they decided to search for help, their only clue being the faint outline of a seemingly abandoned town in the distance.

With no other option, the friends ventured towards the ghost town, which they soon discovered was called Raptor's Hollow. The town appeared to have been abandoned for years, its buildings decaying and overgrown with vines. As they wandered through the desolate streets, an eerie sense of foreboding settled over them.

Their search for help took a gruesome turn when they stumbled upon multiple bodies, their lifeless forms scattered throughout the town. The friends began to panic, realizing that they were in far greater danger than they had initially thought. To make matters worse, they discovered that their cell phones had no reception, leaving them completely cut off from the outside world.

As night fell, the friends were suddenly confronted by a vicious velociraptor, its predatory instincts awakened by the scent of the fresh bodies. With no time to react, the friends quickly realized that their only chance of survival lay in finding a working car battery to escape the nightmare that was Raptor's Hollow.

Desperate and terrified, they split into two groups, with Mark, Jessica, and Noah searching for a battery while Lily and Chloe tried to distract the raptor and keep it at bay. As they scoured the abandoned town for any sign of a functioning vehicle, they found themselves in a deadly game of cat and mouse with the relentless predator.

Mark, Jessica, and Noah frantically searched for a car with a working battery, as the clock ticked down and their lives hung in the balance. Meanwhile, Lily trembled inside a nearby storage container, her heart pounding in her chest as she tried to keep the ravenous creature distracted.

Chloe had disappeared, and a terrified Lily clamped her hand over her mouth, attempting to stifle her breaths as the raptor's sinister silhouette appeared at the container's entrance. It sniffed the air, sensing her presence, its mouth salivating with anticipation. The raptor's powerful jaws glistened with deadly intent as it inched closer, forcing its way inside.

Summoning her last ounce of courage, Lily seized her chance and squeezed through a small rusted hole in the container. In that heart-stopping moment, Chloe reappeared, slamming the container door shut and trapping the velociraptor inside. The two girls clung to each other, their relief short-lived as the enraged raptor thrashed and hissed within its metal prison, its claws scraping against the walls.

The container's lock groaned and bent under the force of the raptor's relentless assault, a grim reminder that their safety was fleeting. Lily and Chloe exchanged a determined glance, knowing they had no choice but to flee before the beast broke free and resumed its merciless pursuit.

As they worked together to install the battery in their car, the raptor broke free and began closing in, its cunning and agility making it a formidable opponent. The friends used every ounce of their strength and ingenuity to fend off the creature, buying themselves just enough time to finish their task.

With the battery in place, they jumped into the car and sped
away from Raptor's Hollow, the raptor's furious screeches
echoing through the night. As they left the ghost town far behind them, the friends couldn't help but shudder at the memory of the horrors they had faced.

The harrowing ordeal in Raptor's Hollow brought the friends
closer together, their bonds forged in the fires of fear and
desperation. They vowed never to speak of the nightmare
they had experienced, the tale of the abandoned town and the
vicious velociraptor becoming a closely guarded secret.

The Thawing Terror

At the fringes of Antarctica, a remote research station found itself in the grip of an unprecedented heatwave. The team of scientists stationed there, led by Dr. Elizabeth Hawkins, struggled to comprehend the rapidly changing conditions and continued to study the effects of climate change on the frozen landscape.

As the ice began to melt at an alarming rate, a shocking discovery was made. Encased within the melting ice was the remarkably preserved body of a prehistoric saber-toothed tiger. The scientists, intrigued by this extraordinary find, decided to study the creature and learn more about its life in a time long past.

However, as the heatwave intensified, the unthinkable occurred. The once-frozen saber-toothed tiger began to stir, its ancient slumber disrupted by the warmth that now engulfed it. The creature's instincts took over, and it awoke with a fierce hunger and a primal drive to survive.

The research team found themselves in mortal danger, as the once-docile specimen transformed into a relentless predator. Led by Dr. Hawkins, the scientists scrambled to protect themselves and the research station from the thawed terror.

Aware that they were ill-equipped to combat such a formidable foe, the team sent out a distress signal, desperately hoping for rescue. With each passing hour, the saber-toothed tiger grew bolder and more cunning, testing the defenses of the station and searching for a weakness to exploit.

Knowing they were running out of defenses, Dr. Harrison, a climatologist, bravely ventured into the station's storage room to retrieve additional supplies for the barricades.

Unbeknownst to him, the saber-toothed tiger had stealthily
infiltrated the room to find food. As he turned to leave, the
creature lunged at him, its fangs sinking into his chest and back.
Hearing his screams, his colleagues rushed to his aid, managing
to drive the beast away with a barrage of makeshift weapons.
But it was too late, Dr. Harrison was severely injured and had
lost too much blood. The team fought valiantly to stem the flow
of blood, but it quickly became apparent that their efforts were
in vain. With each labored breath, the light in Dr. Harrison's
eyes dimmed, and his colleagues knew they were powerless to
save him. Tears streamed down their faces as they listened to
his final, heart-wrenching request: to tell his family that he loved
them dearly and had faced death with courage.

As they huddled around him, offering whispered words of comfort and solace, the air in the room suddenly grew thick with
menace. The door crashed open, and the saber-toothed tiger
re-entered into the room, its eyes locked on Dr. Harrison's lifeless form. The researchers recoiled in horror, unable to process
the macabre scene unfolding before them.

With a blood-curdling snarl, the saber-toothed tiger seized Dr.
Harrison's body in its powerful jaws, dragging him away into
the darkness outside to feast. The team was left with a chilling
reminder of the brutality of their adversary and a renewed determination to survive the nightmarish ordeal.

Later that night, the saber-toothed tiger had managed to breach
their defenses; the researchers found themselves cornered in
the station's dining hall while they were looking for food. The
team, forced to improvise, used chairs and kitchen utensils as
weapons. As the tiger lunged at Dr. Patel, she narrowly evaded
its powerful jaws by diving beneath a table. Simultaneously, Dr.
Thompson swung a heavy frying pan at the tiger's head, stun-
ning it momentarily. Seizing the opportunity, the team retreated
to a safer location within the station, leaving the disoriented

tiger behind.

As the hours turned into days, the team found themselves growing increasingly desperate. They were running low on supplies and their defenses were beginning to falter. Just when all seemed lost, the radio crackled to life with the promise of rescue.

A specialized team had been dispatched to their location, equipped to deal with the prehistoric predator and ensure the safety of the scientists. With renewed hope, the researchers mustered their remaining strength and prepared for a final stand against the saber-toothed tiger.

They turned the central room of the station into a makeshift fortress, reinforcing the doors and windows, and creating an arsenal of improvised weapons from the tools and materials they had left on hand.

The hours ticked away, the tension mounting as they waited for the saber-toothed tiger to make its final move. The silence was deafening, broken only by the occasional howl of the Antarctic winds outside. Each of them knew that their lives were on the line, and the weight of that knowledge hung heavily in the air.

Finally, the attack came. With a guttural snarl and a powerful lunge, the saber-toothed tiger burst through one of the reinforced doors, its eyes burning with predatory rage. The researchers sprang into action, their hearts pounding as adrenaline surged through their veins.

Dr. Patel and Dr. Thompson worked together, attempting to flank the beast and force it into a corner. They wielded their makeshift weapons with grim determination, striking out at the creature whenever they saw an opening. Meanwhile, Dr. Ramirez focused on keeping the tiger's attention divided, hurling objects at it and shouting to distract it from her colleagues.

The battle was brutal and chaotic, a desperate dance of life and death. Despite the team's best efforts, the saber-toothed tiger seemed unstoppable, its powerful muscles propelling it through the room with terrifying agility. At one point, Dr. Thompson was knocked to the ground, the creature's claws just inches from his face as he rolled away in a last-ditch effort to avoid being torn apart.

At that moment the rescue team had finally arrived. They descended upon the scene, armed with high-powered tranquilizer rifles and advanced containment gear. Their faces were a mixture of determination and concern, knowing full well the danger they faced.

As the scientists fought to keep the saber-toothed tiger at bay, the rescuers moved with precision and skill, taking up positions around the room. With nerves of steel, they took aim and fired a barrage of tranquilizer darts into the ferocious beast. The tiger roared in fury, its movements growing increasingly sluggish as the powerful sedatives coursed through its veins.

Despite its fading strength, the creature continued to thrash and snarl, its primal instincts driving it to fight until the bitter end. The rescue team worked swiftly, employing cutting-edge containment techniques to secure the enormous predator. They used reinforced netting and restraints, expertly maneuvering around the tiger's snapping jaws and slashing claws.

With the last of the restraints in place, the once-mighty saber-toothed tiger finally succumbed to the tranquilizers, its massive body slumping to the ground. The entire room seemed to exhale in unison, as both the scientists and the rescuers breathed a collective sigh of relief.

Grateful for their survival and awed by the bravery of their rescuers, the scientists found themselves humbled in the face of such courage and expertise. With the threat neutralized, they could finally begin to process the harrowing ordeal they had endured and pay tribute to the sacrifices made in the name of discovery and survival.

The saber-toothed tiger was carefully transported to a secure facility, where it would be studied and monitored, its existence a testament to the power of nature and the unexpected consequences of a rapidly changing world.

Dr. Hawkins and her team returned to civilization, forever changed by their harrowing experience. They had faced an ancient terror and emerged victorious, their bonds strengthened by adversity and the knowledge that they had survived the wrath of the Thawing Terror.

The Forgotten Forest

Deep within the heart of the ancient Whispering Woods, a sinister secret lay hidden beneath the gnarled branches and twisted roots. Rumors spoke of colossal dinosaur spirits, trapped within the forest, condemned to an eternity of torment and unrest. The spirits were said to be cursed, their once-majestic forms twisted into grotesque and fearsome shapes by the passage of time and the weight of their eternal anguish.

Four friends, Emily, Max, Harper, and Leo, had grown up on the outskirts of the Whispering Woods, fascinated by the legends and drawn to the mysteries that shrouded the ancient forest. United by their curiosity and thirst for adventure, they decided to embark on a quest to uncover the truth behind the cursed dinosaur spirits.

Armed with little more than their courage and a collection of old maps, the friends ventured deep into the heart of the Whispering Woods, guided by the faint whispers of the wind and the eerie cries of the forest's inhabitants. As they delved further into the shadows, they began to feel a palpable sense of dread, as if they were being watched by unseen eyes.

It was not long before they stumbled upon the lair of the cursed spirits, a haunting clearing marked by a circle of ancient, twisted trees. In the center of the clearing stood a massive stone monolith, inscribed with cryptic runes and symbols that seemed to pulse with an otherworldly energy.

As the friends cautiously approached the monolith, they were suddenly confronted by the cursed spirits themselves. Monstrous forms of prehistoric creatures, twisted and distorted by dark magic, emerged from the shadows like nightmares brought to life. A terrifying Velociraptor with elongated, razor-sharp claws and unnaturally glowing red eyes stalked towards them, while a massive Triceratops, its horns twisted and covered in thorny spikes, pawed at the ground menacingly. Above them, a ghostly Pteranodon swooped and screeched, its membranous wings casting eerie shadows across the moonlit landscape.

The friends stood their ground, their hearts pounding with terror and awe as they faced the fearsome creatures. In a split-second decision, they knew they had to run. They scattered in different directions, hoping to confuse the cursed spirits and buy themselves some time.

Max sprinted through the twisted undergrowth, the sound of the Triceratops' heavy footsteps and labored breathing right behind him. He knew he couldn't outrun the beast forever, so he made a desperate leap into a narrow crevice between two large boulders, wedging himself in tightly. The Triceratops charged, slamming its horned head into the rocks, but Max was just out of reach.

Meanwhile, Leo found himself pursued by the Velociraptor, its unearthly hissing and snarling filling his ears as it closed in on him. He tried to scramble up a steep incline, but the cursed spirit was too quick. With a final, desperate lunge, the Velociraptor snatched Leo in its powerful jaws, dragging him away screaming for help.

Harper and Emily knew they had to regroup and rescue Leo and Max, but they also understood the daunting task ahead of them. They would have to confront the cursed spirits head-on and somehow break the ancient curse that had brought these monstrous dinosaurs back to life.

Dodging the attacks of the Pteranodon, suddenly remembering a fragment of the ancient legend, Emily recalled that the

spirits could only be freed from their curse by the power of forgiveness and a selfless act of love. Desperate to save both themselves and their friends, they clasped hands and bravely stood in front of the monolith, their voices joining together in a heartfelt plea for forgiveness and understanding as they began to chant the mysterious words etched into the stone, their voices resonating through the eerie silence:

"Ospiras lumina, noctis terminus,
Tenebrae vincant, spiritus redemptio.
Aeternae catenae, nunc frangantur,
Ab origine mundi, ad finem temporis."

These ancient words, believed to be a long-lost language, roughly translated to:
"Spirits of light, end the night,
Let darkness be conquered, redemption take flight.
Eternal chains, now be shattered,
From the world's beginning, to the end of time."

As they spoke the words of the ancient ritual, they felt a surge of energy coursing through them, an otherworldly power connecting them to the very fabric of the universe. They knew, deep within their souls, that they were invoking an ancient magic powerful enough to break the curse, freeing the tormented spirits of the dinosaurs and saving their friends.

And it began to work, the monolith began to glow with a radiant light, its power growing stronger with each syllable. The cursed dinosaurs were drawn to the light, the Triceratops leaving Max, the Velociraptor dropping the injured Leo, the Pteranodon stopping its attack to land beside them. Their grotesque forms bathed in the gentle glow of the monolith. As the friends watched, the spirits began to transform, their twisted bodies reverting to their once-majestic forms, the torment and pain that had haunted them for so long finally washed away.

With the curse broken, the spirits of the dinosaurs were at last
free to find peace, their ethereal forms vanishing into the wind
as they departed the Whispering Woods. The friends were
left standing in the clearing, the weight of their accomplish-
ment settling upon them as they realized that they had not only
survived their encounter with the cursed spirits, but had also
played a part in their redemption.

The friends returned to their village as heroes, their tale of
bravery and compassion spreading far and wide. The legend
of the cursed spirits lived on, but it was no longer a story of
fear and despair. Instead, it became a testament to the power
of love, forgiveness, and the indomitable spirit of friendship.

Emily, Max, Harper, and Leo continued to explore the mysteries of the Whispering Woods and the world beyond, their
bond forged by their shared adventure and the knowledge that
they had faced the unknown together and triumphed. And as
they journeyed on, the memory of the Forgotten Forest and
the spirits they had freed would remain with them, a constant
reminder of the incredible power of love and forgiveness.

The Shadow Beneath the Cliffs

In the quaint seaside town of Fossil Cove, a long-forgotten tale of terror had been buried beneath the waves for centuries. The legend spoke of a monstrous aquatic dinosaur, known as the Shadow, that was said to rise from the depths during the stormiest of nights, seeking vengeance for its untimely demise.

Three childhood friends, Mia, Lucas, and Oliver, had always been fascinated by the mysterious legend. Their adventurous spirits and insatiable curiosity drew them to the rocky cliffs that bordered the town, where they hoped to uncover the truth behind the ancient tale.

One stormy evening, as thunder rumbled in the distance, the friends decided to brave the tempest and journey to the cliffs, armed with nothing but their courage and a few flashlights. As they trekked along the shoreline, the waves crashed against the rocks with a ferocity that seemed almost supernatural.

As they neared the cliffs, an eerie silence settled over the landscape, the storm momentarily abating. Suddenly, a chilling roar echoed through the night, and the friends realized with a mixture of fear and awe that the Shadow was near.

They scrambled to find cover, hiding behind a large boulder as the monstrous creature emerged from the churning waters. The aquatic dinosaur towered over them, its scales shimmering with an otherworldly light, its eyes filled with an ancient rage. The Mosasaurus snapped its massive jaws, razor-sharp teeth gleaming in the moonlight, and let out a guttural roar that shook the very earth beneath their feet.

Mia, Lucas, and Oliver knew they had to act quickly if they

were to survive the encounter. As the Mosasaurus began to thrash its massive tail, causing waves to crash around them, they devised a plan.

Oliver noticed a nearby cave entrance just beyond the boulder they were hiding behind. It seemed just large enough for them to fit through, but too small for the Mosasaurus to follow.

Taking a deep breath, Mia whispered to Lucas and Oliver, "We need to make a run for that cave. It's our only chance. On the count of three, okay?" They nodded in agreement, their hearts pounding in their chests. "One... two... three!"

The three friends burst from their hiding spot, sprinting toward the cave entrance as the enraged Mosasaurus spotted them. The creature lunged forward, snapping its jaws mere inches from Mia's heels. They could feel the ground shake with each powerful stroke of the Mosasaurus' tail, the air thick with the scent of its breath, a mixture of saltwater and decaying flesh.

With adrenaline pumping through their veins, Mia, Lucas, and Oliver dove into the narrow cave entrance, narrowly avoiding the snapping jaws of the Mosasaurus. As the creature roared in frustration, its massive body slammed against the cave entrance, causing rocks to tumble and begin to block the entrance.

Breathing heavily, the friends huddled together in the darkness of the cave, knowing they had just escaped certain death by mere inches but it wasn't over as the ancient sea creature continued its hunger induced slams against the exterior of the cave.

Remembering a local myth that stated the creature could be appeased by the sound of a pure and innocent melody, Mia began to whistle a simple tune she had learned as a child.Her friends confused tried to make her stop but the haunting notes of her melody seemed to resonate with the creature, as it paused and

tilted its head, as if listening intently. The friends watched in amazement as the monstrous dinosaur's eyes softened, its rage giving way to a sense of peace.

As Mia continued to whistle, the creature lowered its head and allowed the friends to approach. They hesitantly reached out and touched its scales, feeling a strange connection to the ancient beast.

With the storm subsiding, the Shadow returned to the depths, leaving the friends with a profound sense of wonder and gratitude. They knew they had experienced something few people had ever witnessed and had formed a bond with a creature that had long been feared and misunderstood.

Mia, Lucas, and Oliver returned to Fossil Cove with a newfound appreciation for the mysteries of the world and the power of empathy and understanding. The legend of the Shadow Beneath the Cliffs took on a new meaning, no longer a story of terror but rather one of hope and redemption.

The Unseen Echoes

The small coastal town of Murkshore had a dark secret, one that had been buried for centuries beneath the shifting sands and forgotten by time. It was said that the restless spirits of prehistoric dinosaurs still wandered the beaches, trapped between life and death, cursed to roam the earth for eternity.

Three friends, Riley, Noah, and Lily, had grown up in Murkshore and had heard the stories of the ghostly dinosaurs all their lives. They were intrigued by the legends and longed to know the truth behind the mysterious hauntings. So, one foggy autumn evening, they decided to venture out to the beach to uncover the secrets hidden beneath the sands.

As they walked along the shoreline, the dense fog seemed to come alive, swirling around them like tendrils of an ancient, unseen force. The waves crashed against the shore, their rhythmic song a haunting melody that sent chills down their spines.

Suddenly, they stumbled upon a series of unearthly footprints, deeply embedded in the sand. The tracks appeared to be made by a large, bipedal dinosaur, one that had long been extinct. The friends cautiously followed the prints, each step taking them deeper into the foggy abyss.

As they ventured further along the beach, they began to hear strange, otherworldly sounds echoing through the night. The low, guttural roars and haunting cries sent shivers down their spines, as they realized they were not alone. The ghostly dinosaurs were near, their presence felt in the eerie whispers of the wind and the chilling echoes that seemed to surround them.

The friends found themselves standing at the edge of an an-

cient graveyard, the final resting place of countless prehistoric creatures. The unearthly footprints led them to a massive, partially unearthed dinosaur skeleton, its enormous bones protruding from the sand like a macabre monument to a forgotten past.

As the fog grew denser, the ghostly dinosaurs began to materialize around them, their spectral forms barely visible in the swirling mists. Riley, Noah, and Lily stood their ground, their hearts pounding with a mixture of fear and fascination.

Remembering an old legend that had been passed down through generations, Lily recalled a story about a ghostly sea captain who once protected the beach. According to the legend, the captain's spirit could be summoned in times of great need. Desperate for help, Lily shouted the captain's name, "Captain Nathaniel Blackthorne, we need your help!"

As her plea echoed through the night, the ghostly figure of Captain Blackthorne materialized before them, his ethereal form shrouded in a tattered, salt-stained cloak. He raised his spectral cutlass and shouted, "Stand back, young ones! Let me deal with these ancient beasts!"

The ghostly dinosaurs, which included the towering forms of a spectral T-Rex, a pack of phantom Velociraptors, and the long-necked, ghostly apparition of an Apatosaurus, surrounded the friends, their otherworldly roars sending chills down their spines. The spectral T-Rex lunged at them, but Captain Blackthorne intercepted it, slashing with his ghostly cutlass and forcing the ancient creature to recoil.

The ghostly Velociraptors attacked in a coordinated frenzy, but the sea captain fought them off with a series of agile movements and swift, calculated strikes. Captain Blackthorne even stood his ground against the enormous Apatosaurus, using his cunning and experience to dodge its powerful, sweeping tail and ghostly stomps.

As Captain Blackthorne fended off the spectral dinosaurs, he called out to the friends, "Now's your chance! Run while I hold them off!" Riley, Noah, and Lily didn't hesitate, sprinting away from the ghostly confrontation, their hearts pounding in their chests.

The friends reached a safe distance, pausing to catch their breath and glance back at the beach. The ghostly sea captain fought valiantly, eventually driving the ancient spirits back into the depths of the fog. With a final salute, Captain Blackthorne faded into the night, his duty fulfilled.

The legend of the ghostly dinosaurs and Captain Blackthorne lived on in Murkshore, but it was no longer a tale of fear and dread. Instead, it became a story of hope and redemption, a testament to the power of courage and the resilience of the human spirit.

Riley, Noah, and Lily continued to explore the mysteries of their small coastal town, their bond strengthened by their shared experience. They knew that they had witnessed something truly extraordinary that night, and they would carry the memory of the Unseen Echoes with them for the rest of their lives.

The Raptor's Lullaby

In the remote village of Clawton, nestled in the shadow of an ancient mountain range, a chilling legend had haunted the townspeople for generations. It was said that deep within the heart of the mountains lay a hidden valley, home to a pack of ghostly velociraptors that roamed the land by night, preying on the souls of those who strayed too close to their lair.

The villagers spoke in hushed tones of the Raptor's Lullaby, a haunting melody that echoed through the mountains, luring the unsuspecting to their doom. Despite the numerous warnings and tales of terror, four friends—Zoe, Jack, Ava, and Sam—found themselves drawn to the legend. They were determined to uncover the truth behind the mysterious valley and its ghostly inhabitants.

Armed with a hand-drawn map they had found in an old library, the friends embarked on a daring expedition into the heart of the mountains. The air grew colder as they climbed higher, the eerie silence of the landscape broken only by the distant howl of the wind. As night fell, they made camp in a small clearing, huddling around a fire for warmth and comfort.

In the dead of night, as the moon cast its ghostly glow over the mountain peaks, a haunting melody drifted through the air. The Raptor's Lullaby had begun. The friends exchanged nervous glances, feeling a strange mixture of excitement and terror. They knew that the legend was true, and they were closer than ever to uncovering the hidden valley.

Following the haunting melody, they ventured deeper into the mountains, their flashlights casting eerie shadows on the jagged cliffs. The lullaby grew louder and more hypnotic, leading them to a narrow passage hidden behind a veil of ivy.

As they squeezed through the passage, the world around them seemed to change. The air was thick with an otherworldly mist, and the moon cast an unnatural glow on the landscape. The friends realized that they had entered the realm of the ghostly raptors.

They cautiously ventured into the valley, searching for any signs of the spectral creatures. The lullaby was now a powerful, enchanting chorus that seemed to echo from every corner of the valley. Suddenly, the ghostly raptors appeared, their translucent forms shimmering in the moonlight.

Zoe, Jack, Ava, and Sam stood frozen in fear as the raptors circled them, their eerie song growing louder and more hypnotic. The friends felt themselves being drawn deeper into the raptors' spell, their minds clouded by the haunting melody.

Suddenly the spectral creatures lunged at them, their eerie cries echoing through the ravine. With quick thinking, Ava grabbed a nearby rock and threw it at the nearest raptor, dispersing it into a cloud of mist. The friends scrambled out of the rocky area, their hearts pounding as they narrowly escaped the relentless pursuit of the ghostly raptors.

Unable to go back and unsure what to do, the group decided to push forward as they came across a fast-flowing river, the only way to cross being a dilapidated rope bridge. Knowing they had no other option, they decided to take their chances. With Jack in the lead, they carefully stepped onto the swaying bridge, gripping the frayed ropes tightly. Just as they reached the halfway point, the ghostly raptors appeared once more, swooping down and trying to cut the ropes with their sharp talons. The bridge lurched and shook, threatening to send the friends plummeting into the raging river below. Sam bravely swung at the raptors

with a stick he had found earlier, doing his best to ward them off. The group managed to cross the bridge just in time, as it collapsed behind them, the ghostly raptors screeching in frustration.

Their relief was short-lived, however, as they soon found themselves at the edge of a deep ravine, filled with thick fog and eerie whispers. With no other path available, they reluctantly descended into the ravine. The ghostly raptors pursued them relentlessly, their spectral forms seeming to materialize out of the fog itself. As the friends navigated the narrow ledges and treacherous drops, the raptors attacked from all sides, their glowing eyes and ghostly forms becoming indistinguishable from the swirling mists. At one heart-stopping moment, Zoe slipped on a damp rock, barely managing to cling to the edge as a raptor lunged for him. Ava quickly reached out and pulled her to safety, the raptor's jaws snapping shut mere inches from her face. The group pressed on, fighting their way through the haunted ravine, determined to escape the relentless torment of the ghostly raptors.

Deep in the valley, the group found themselves trapped, with no escape route or place to hide from the relentless ghostly raptors. The dense fog and jagged cliffs around them only served to amplify their terror. Jack and Sam, armed with rocks and sticks, bravely positioned themselves between the spectral beasts and Zoe and Ava, who clung to each other, their eyes wide with fear and tears streaming down their faces. They knew, deep down, that this might be the end of their adventure, and possibly their lives.

The ghostly raptors closed in, their eerie cries echoing through the valley as they circled their prey. Jack and Sam, their hearts pounding in their chests, swung their makeshift weapons, trying to hold the terrifying creatures at bay. The raptors lunged, their ghostly forms shimmering and disappearing only to reappear even closer, their razor-sharp claws and teeth mere inches away from the group. Zoe and Ava held their breath, trying to stifle their sobs as they watched Jack and Sam fighting desperately for their lives, knowing that the slightest misstep could mean the end for all of them. The intensity of the situation reached a fever pitch, with the ghostly raptors continuing to torment the group, their relentless pursuit and thirst for fear driving them forward.

In a moment of clarity, Zoe remembered a line from the ancient text they had found in the library: "Only the pure of heart can break the raptor's spell." Desperate to save her friends, she began to sing a heartfelt lullaby her mother had sung to her as a child.

Her pure, melodic voice cut through the raptor's haunting chorus, weakening their spell. The ghostly raptors hissed and screeched, their translucent forms flickering like a dying flame. Zoe's lullaby grew stronger, filling the valley with a warm, soothing light.

The raptors, unable to withstand the power of her song, vanished into the night, their haunting melody silenced forever. The friends felt the enchantment lift, their minds clear and their hearts filled with a newfound courage.

Together, they made their way back to the village, their spirits soaring with the knowledge that they had faced the legendary ghostly raptors and survived. The villagers, who had feared the worst, welcomed them back as heroes, grateful for their bravery in dispelling the ancient curse.

The Cursed Amber

In the quaint town of Amber Hollow, nestled at the foot of an ancient volcano, there was a legend about a rare piece of amber that contained a dark secret. The amber, known as the Cursed Amber, was said to hold the spirit of a ferocious dinosaur that once roamed the land, causing chaos and destruction wherever it went.

Three friends, Emma, Max, and Ben, had grown up hearing stories about the Cursed Amber, but they never believed them. They were fascinated by dinosaurs and often explored the nearby forest, hoping to find fossils or other traces of the prehistoric creatures.

One fateful summer day, while scouring the forest for dinosaur relics, Emma stumbled upon a glint of orange hidden beneath a pile of leaves. She dug it out and found a large, beautifully preserved piece of amber. Inside, the perfect silhouette of a dinosaur was visible, frozen in time.

The friends marveled at the rare find, but they couldn't shake the feeling that there was something unsettling about it. They decided to take it to Mr. Wilson, an old paleontologist who lived on the outskirts of Amber Hollow. He had dedicated his life to studying dinosaurs and was known for his extensive collection of fossils and artifacts.

Upon seeing the amber, Mr. Wilson's eyes widened in fear. He warned the friends that they had found the legendary Cursed Amber and urged them to return it to where they had found it. He told them that the dinosaur trapped within was a malevolent spirit that would bring destruction to anyone who possessed the amber.

Emma, Max, and Ben, skeptical of the old man's claims, decided to keep the amber as a trophy of their discovery. That night, they gathered in Emma's treehouse to examine the amber more closely. As they stared at the dinosaur encased within, they noticed that its eyes seemed to be glowing faintly.

At the stroke of midnight, a powerful storm began to brew outside, the wind howling and lightning illuminating the dark sky. The amber started to vibrate, and a low, haunting growl echoed from within. The friends exchanged nervous glances, suddenly realizing that Mr. Wilson's warnings might have been more than just superstition.

The amber shattered, releasing the sinister dinosaur spirit. It materialized before them, a terrifying creature with razor-sharp teeth and glowing red eyes. The friends screamed and fled the treehouse, the monstrous dinosaur in pursuit.

The creature rampaged through Amber Hollow, its powerful roars shaking the town to its core. The friends knew they had to find a way to stop the dinosaur and save their town from utter destruction.

They sought out Mr. Wilson, who reluctantly agreed to help them. He explained that the only way to defeat the dinosaur spirit was to find a new piece of amber, one that had been formed by the same ancient volcano, and use it to trap the creature once more.

The friends ventured into the heart of the forest, following the paleontologist's directions to the ancient volcanic site. They searched for hours, battling the storm and their own mounting fears. Just as they were about to give up, Ben spotted a glimmer of orange on the ground.

They took the new piece of amber and raced back to Amber

Hollow, where the dinosaur spirit was wreaking havoc.

As they entered the town, they saw the chaos and destruction left in the wake of the dinosaur spirit's rampage. Buildings had been reduced to rubble, cars were overturned, and the once-peaceful streets were now filled with terrified locals running for their lives.

The spirit, in the form of a massive, ghostly Allosaurus, roared and thrashed its powerful tail, shattering windows and leaving deep gouges in the ground. Its eyes, burning with an unearthly fire, seemed to seek out anything that dared to challenge its wrath.

As the friends took in the scene before them, they knew they had to act quickly to save the town and its people. They split up, each using their knowledge of Amber Hollow to assist the people in finding shelter and tending to the injured.

While Max and Ben worked to create a barricade to slow the spirit's rampage, Emma tried to reason with the angry dinosaur, attempting to reach the creature's soul and help it find peace. She stood bravely before the towering Allosaurus, her voice unwavering as she pleaded with it to let go of its rage and find solace in the knowledge that it was not alone in the world.

The Allosaurus hesitated for a moment, its fiery eyes locked on Emma, and the townspeople held its breath. But the spirit's fury could not be easily quelled, and with a thunderous roar, it lunged at Emma, determined to snuff out the human's defiance.

It was then that Max and Ben, having finished constructing their makeshift barrier, rushed to her aid. Armed with the knowledge of the cursed amber and the power it held over the spirit, they joined their friend in confronting the vengeful

Allosaurus, determined to save Amber Hollow and free the
tormented dinosaur spirit from its curse.

Together they held the amber up and began reciting the
ancient spell that Mr. Wilson had taught them. Something
started to happen.

The dinosaur roared in fury, lunging at the friends. They held
their ground, focusing all their energy on the incantation.
A bolt of lightning struck the amber, causing it to glow with
an otherworldly energy. The dinosaur spirit was drawn into
the amber, its roars and snarls fading until it was once again
trapped within the golden resin.

The storm subsided, and the once-rampaging Allosaurus spirit
was now frozen inside the new piece of amber, its red eyes
dimmed and lifeless. The friends breathed a sigh of relief,
knowing that they had saved Amber Hollow from certain
destruction.

They returned to Mr. Wilson's house to inform him of their
victory. He praised their bravery and resourcefulness, but
warned them that the Cursed Amber should never fall into the
wrong hands again. He offered to keep it safe in his collection,
ensuring that the dinosaur spirit would remain trapped for
eternity.

The friends agreed, knowing that the amber would be secure
with the old paleontologist. They thanked him and returned
home, forever changed by their harrowing adventure. The legend of the Cursed Amber became a cautionary tale in Amber
Hollow, passed down through generations to remind people of
the dangers that lurked beneath the surface of the earth.

Fossil Ridge's Hidden Curse

Once, in the small town of Fossil Ridge, there was a group of adventurous kids who loved to explore the local woods. Alan, the most curious of the group, discovered an old map in his grandfather's attic. It was a weathered piece of parchment that showed a hidden cave deep within the woods, supposedly filled with ancient dinosaur bones. Fascinated by the discovery, Alan convinced his friends, Sarah, Mark, and Lily, to venture into the woods and search for the mysterious cave.

The group set off on their expedition on a foggy Saturday morning. The woods were filled with an eerie silence, broken only by the distant hooting of an owl. The thick mist swirled around them, hiding the towering trees from their sight. The deeper they ventured, the more uneasy they felt, as if someone—or something—was watching them.

Finally, they arrived at the entrance of the cave. The walls were adorned with strange symbols that none of them could decipher. Mark, the bravest among them, led the way inside, flashlight in hand. The cave was damp and cold, the smell of mold and decay filling the air. As they descended deeper into the darkness, they noticed that the cave walls were now covered in ancient paintings of giant reptilian creatures. Their uneasiness grew, but their curiosity drove them forward.

Suddenly, they stumbled upon a large chamber filled with colossal dinosaur skeletons. Massive rib cages protruding from the earth, skulls of Tyrannosaurus Rex, Triceratops and more. The fossils loomed over them, casting eerie shadows on the walls. Sarah gasped as she saw something move in the corner of her eye. She turned around, but there was nothing there. She dismissed it as her imagination playing tricks on her.

The group continued to explore the chamber, marveling at the terrifying creatures that once ruled the Earth. Mark found a partially buried skull, and as he brushed off the dirt, the skull's eye sockets started to glow a menacing red. The entire chamber began to shake, as if it were alive. A guttural growl echoed throughout the cave, sending shivers down their spines.

The dinosaur skeletons started to come alive, their bones rattling and shifting as they re-assembled themselves. The kids' eyes widened in terror as the skeletal dinosaurs towered above them, their glowing red eyes piercing the darkness. The bony T-Rex roared, shaking the very ground they stood on. A Triceratops dug out the ground, gearing up to charge. A group of Compsognathus, chirped at each other almost coordinating their attack.

In a panic, the friends sprinted back towards the cave entrance. They stumbled and tripped over rocks, their heartbeats pounding in their ears. The skeletal dinosaurs pursued them, their massive strides echoing like thunder in the cavern. The cave seemed to stretch on endlessly, the exit nowhere in sight.

Sarah stumbled and fell, her ankle twisting violently beneath her, pain shooting up her leg. Alan, Mark, and Lily skidded to a halt to help her, but the ghostly dinosaurs were bearing down on them, their eyes blazing with a terrifying, otherworldly hunger.

The T-Rex lunged at them, its massive jaws snapping inches from their faces. Lily, thinking quickly, snatched a jagged rock from the ground and hurled it at the beast's glowing eye. The rock struck true, and the T-Rex reared back, disoriented and screeching in pain. The chaos provided an opening for the Triceratops to charge. Its enormous horns, easily six feet long, aimed to impale the group, promising a gruesome fate.

In a last-ditch effort, they dove out of the way just in time,

causing the Triceratops to collide with the cave wall. The impact was earth-shattering, and the cave began to crumble around them.

Seizing the opportunity, Mark hoisted Sarah onto his shoulder, and they all sprinted towards the exit, the sounds of destruction echoing behind them. The cave's ceiling collapsed, rocks and debris raining down as the Triceratops shook off its failed attack. The T-Rex, along with the pack of Compsognathus, rapidly gained on them, their skeletal forms creating a deafening sound of scraping and crunching as they ran.

The light from the cave entrance grew closer, but the Compsognathus leaped into the air, their small but razor-sharp talons outstretched, eager to sink into their prey. Just as the creatures were about to strike, the cave entrance collapsed, sealing the skeletal dinosaurs inside, leaving the friends in a cloud of dust and debris, their hearts pounding with terror and relief.

The friends collapsed on the forest floor, gasping for breath. They looked back at the cave, now hidden beneath a mound of rubble. They knew they had just escaped an ancient curse, but they couldn't shake the feeling that the dinosaurs' spirits still lingered in the shadows of Fossil Ridge.

As they limped back to town, they vowed never to speak of their harrowing experience. But every night, as they lay in their beds, they could still hear the distant roar of the skeletal T-Rex, a chilling reminder of the terror they had faced. The once curious and adventurous kids now avoided the woods, fearing the return of the haunting dino shadows.

Word spread throughout Fossil Ridge about the cave's collapse, but nobody knew the truth behind it. The town eventually returned to its usual, quiet routine. The kids, however, could never forget the horrifying creatures that had come to life right before their eyes.

The Forest of Ancient Predators

Ben and his son, Max, shared a passion for exploring the great outdoors. One weekend, they decided to embark on a hiking adventure, eager to bond and discover the hidden treasures of the wilderness.

Their journey led them to a mysterious, dark forest, its entrance partially concealed by overgrown vegetation. Intrigued, they decided to venture inside, armed with their flashlights and a sense of wonder.

As they delved deeper into the forest, they stumbled upon a chilling sight: piles of bones and flesh sitting in pools of blood, evidence of some long-forgotten predator that still called this forest home. Unsettled but undeterred, they pressed on, determined to uncover the secrets of this eerie place.

Deeper into the dark and dense forest, the father and son reached winding paths and shadowy corners which soon separated them, leaving Max alone and frightened. Max wandered through the shadowy forest, searching for his father, as the air grew colder, and a palpable sense of dread began to envelop him.

The eerie silence was punctuated by the distant sound of snapping branches and rustling leaves. Max's heart raced, and he desperately called out for his father, but there was still no response.

As Max rounded a bend in the winding path, he caught sight of something that made his blood run cold. Partially obscured by the dense foliage, he saw a pair of unblinking, reptilian eyes staring at him from the darkness. The eyes were unnervingly

large and belonged to a creature unlike anything Max had ever seen before.

A Deinosuchus slowly emerged from the shadows, revealing its monstrous form. The 35-foot-long prehistoric crocodile was an intimidating sight, its massive jaws bristling with rows of razor-sharp teeth. The beast's powerful tail dragged along the ground, its scales glistening with an otherworldly sheen in the moonlight.

Max was frozen in terror, his breath caught in his throat as the Deinosuchus began to advance towards him, its eyes locked on its prey. The creature's footsteps caused the ground to tremble, and each exhaled breath was accompanied by a guttural growl that shook Max to his core.

Inch by inch, the Deinosuchus drew closer, its enormous mouth opening wide as it prepared to strike. Max's mind raced, searching for a way to escape, but he found himself paralyzed by fear.

Just as the Deinosuchus lunged, Ben appeared from the shadows, hurling rocks and shouting to distract the beast and divert its attention from his son. The crocodile hesitated for a moment, its attention momentarily drawn away from Max, providing a crucial window of opportunity for them to escape.

Seizing the opportunity, Max sprinted towards the forest entrance, his heart pounding with fear and gratitude for his father's courageous act. He reached the daylight, breathless and shaken, as the sounds of the struggle between his father and the Deinosuchus echoed through the trees.

Fearing the worst, Max stood at the edge of the forest, tears streaming down his face. He was certain that his father had sacrificed himself to save him from the jaws of the ancient predator. Minutes passed, each one feeling like an eternity as Max mourned the loss of his father.

Suddenly, Ben emerged from the forest, his clothes tattered and covered in blood, but alive. Max's eyes widened in disbelief and relief as he embraced his father, grateful beyond words for his bravery and love.

The father and son duo quickly retreated from the forest, leaving the Deinosuchus and the grim secrets of the woods behind. Their harrowing experience had brought them closer than ever, a powerful reminder of the bond they shared and the lengths to which they would go to protect one another.

Their tale of survival and courage in the face of unimaginable danger became a family legend, passed down through generations as a testament to the power of love and the resilience of the human spirit.

The Nightmarish Chimera Experiment

Dr. Samuel Whitmore was a brilliant yet unhinged scientist, driven by an insatiable desire to unlock the secrets of life itself. His obsession led him down a path of darkness, experimenting with the manipulation of DNA to create entirely new species. Unbeknownst to the world, Dr. Whitmore's latest project involved splicing the DNA of a tiger with that of an Ambopteryx, a species of dinosaur that had bat-like membrane wings, hoping to create a monstrous, prehistoric hybrid.

Meanwhile, a group of college students, eager for excitement and adventure, decided to sneak into Dr. Whitmore's isolated laboratory. They had heard rumors of the mad scientist's experiments and were curious to see for themselves what lay hidden within the walls of his secretive facility.

As they entered the dimly lit lab, the students were confronted with a horrifying sight: Dr. Whitmore's lifeless body, sprawled across the floor, covered in deep gashes and surrounded by broken glass and overturned equipment. The shock quickly turned to terror as they realized that the abomination he had created was on the loose.

The monstrous hybrid, which they dubbed the "Chimerasaur," was a grotesque blend of tiger and giant bat. It had the powerful limbs and razor-sharp claws of a tiger, combined with the massive wings and nightmarish features of a giant reptilian bat. As it stalked the corridors of the laboratory, its chilling screech and guttural growls echoed through the building.

The students knew that they had to escape the laboratory before the Chimerasaur found them. They split up, each one searching for a way out while avoiding the deadly predator.

The once-silent halls were now filled with the echoing cries of the creature and the frantic footsteps of the terrified students. As they navigated the labyrinthine facility, the students discovered the disturbing extent of Dr. Whitmore's experiments. The laboratory was filled with an array of grotesque chimeras, each more horrifying than the last, left to die in their cages and tanks. These twisted results of the scientist's relentless pursuit of knowledge seemed to defy the laws of nature.

In one corner, a creature with the body of a venomous snake and the legs of a giant spider skittered across the floor, its fangs dripping with lethal venom. In another area, a monstrosity with the head of a piranha and the lower body of a scorpion scuttled about, its tail poised to strike with deadly accuracy while its many rows of teeth chatter in hunger.

In yet another enclosure, a bizarre combination of a gorilla and a giant octopus loomed. It had the muscular arms and torso of a gorilla, but instead of legs, it had eight powerful tentacles that allowed it to move with surprising speed and agility. Its eyes were unsettlingly human-like, seeming to gaze into the souls of those who encountered it.

In the darkest corner of the lab, a chimera that was part bear and part giant eagle lay in wait. It had the massive, furry body of a bear, but its wings were covered in razor-sharp feathers, capable of slicing through flesh with ease. Its beak was large enough to snap a human in half, and its piercing eyes gleamed with predatory intelligence.

Each of these creatures was a testament to Dr. Whitmore's twisted genius and boundless ambition. He had pushed the limits of science and ethics, creating beings that should never have existed. The students couldn't help but shudder in revulsion and fear as they traversed the laboratory, encountering one nightmarish chimera after another.

CHIMERA

As the students cautiously made their way through the horrifying menagerie of twisted chimeras, they stumbled upon Dr. Whitmore's control room. The dimly lit chamber was filled with monitors displaying the various creatures and their enclosures. Amidst the complex array of buttons, switches, and dials, Mike noticed a large, red button hidden beneath a protective cover.

Upon further examination, they discovered that the button was labeled "Self-Destruct Sequence." It seemed that, in his madness, Dr. Whitmore had installed a fail-safe to destroy his laboratory and the abominations it contained. The students exchanged nervous glances, each one silently considering the implications of activating the self-destruct sequence.

"We have to do it," Sarah whispered, her voice trembling. "These creatures... they're not natural. They're suffering, and they're dangerous. If we don't end this now, who knows what could happen if they escape?"

The others nodded in agreement, understanding the gravity of the situation. With a heavy heart, Tom lifted the protective cover and pressed the self-destruct button. A robotic voice immediately blared through the speakers, announcing the activation of the self-destruct sequence and counting down from ten minutes.

As the countdown began, the students scrambled to escape the laboratory before it was reduced to rubble. They could hear the panicked roars and cries of the chimeras as they sensed the impending doom. As much as they pitied the creatures, the students knew that setting them free would have unleashed untold horrors upon the world.

The students made their way through the labyrinthine corridors of the laboratory racing towards the exit. Suddenly, they found themselves face-to-face with the Chimerasaur once more. The monstrous hybrid was enraged, aware of its impending doom, and it seemed intent on taking the students down with it.

Realizing that they would have to work together if they hoped to escape, the students quickly formulated a plan. Each of them would use their unique skills to distract, evade, and outmaneuver the Chimerasaur, buying them precious time to make their escape.

Sarah, the quick-thinking biology major, acted first. She grabbed a vial of potent chemicals from a nearby shelf and hurled it at the Chimerasaur. The vial shattered upon impact, releasing a noxious cloud that momentarily disoriented the creature, causing it to stagger and roar in confusion.

Seizing the opportunity, Tom, the resourceful engineering student, rushed to the nearest electrical panel. He quickly rewired the circuits, diverting power to a set of overhead lights. With a flick of a switch, he flooded the area with a blinding light, further disorienting the Chimerasaur and buying them more time to escape.

Meanwhile, Lisa, the agile psychology major, sprinted towards the beast. Just as it shook off the effects of the bright light, she deftly leaped over its snapping jaws, drawing its attention away from her friends. As the Chimerasaur pursued her, she nimbly dodged its every attack, her agility and quick reflexes keeping her just out of reach of its deadly claws and teeth.

Finally, Mike, the cunning computer science major, took advantage of the chaos to access the laboratory's security system once more. He quickly located the controls for the automated fire suppression system and activated it, filling the room with a dense cloud of fire-retardant foam. The Chimerasaur, already

disoriented from the combined efforts of the students, was
now completely blinded and disoriented.

With the Chimerasaur temporarily neutralized, the students
regrouped and made their way towards the exit. The alarms
continued to blare, and the countdown relentlessly ticked away
as they raced through the corridors, their hearts pounding
with fear and adrenaline. They could hear the Chimerasaur's
enraged roars echoing through the halls, a chilling reminder of
the danger that still lurked within the laboratory's walls.

And just as the countdown reached its final seconds, the
students burst through the entrance and sprinted to a safe
distance. They watched in a mixture of awe and relief as the
laboratory exploded in a massive fireball, consuming the twisted creations within. The ground shook beneath their feet as
the remnants of Dr. Whitmore's life's work crumbled to dust.
Their harrowing experience had left them shaken but alive,
their lives forever changed by the horrors they had witnessed.

The story of the Chimerasaur and the mad scientist's twisted
experiments remained a closely guarded secret, known only to
the survivors and those who dared to explore the abandoned
laboratory. A chilling reminder of the dangers of unchecked
ambition and the darker side of scientific curiosity, the tale
of Dr. Whitmore's chimera serves as a warning to those who
seek to manipulate the very fabric of life.

The Night at La Brea Tar Pits

On a warm summer night, a young couple named Emily and Brian decided to sneak into the La Brea Tar Pits for a romantic adventure. The moonlit park had an eerie allure, and they thought it would be thrilling to explore the forbidden grounds after hours.

Hand in hand, they tiptoed through the shadows, eventually finding a secluded spot near the bubbling tar pits. As Brian leaned in for a kiss an odd noise abruptly echoed around them. The tar pits began to boil loudly, the thick black substance churning and frothing as if something was about to emerge.

Suddenly, the ground beneath their feet began to rumble, sending tremors through the park. In an instant, a monstrous, hairless woolly mammoth burst forth from the tar pits, its burned and scarred flesh a horrifying testament to its torment. Its eyes, devoid of warmth or life, seemed possessed by something malevolent and ancient.

Terrified, Emily and Brian scrambled to escape the relentless pursuit of the monstrous beast. The mammoth charged after them, its unearthly shrieks and thundering footsteps filling the night with dread.

As they ran through the park, the mammoth's monstrous form crashed through trees and smashed benches in its pursuit, its eyes locked on the terrified couple.

Brian and Emily stumbled upon a construction site where the park was undergoing renovations. With no other options, they dashed between the towering stacks of wooden beams, hoping

to outmaneuver the mammoth. The beast, however, refused to be deterred, its massive tusks tearing through the wood like paper. It seemed to predict their every move, driving them further into the maze of obstacles.

In a heart-stopping moment, Emily tripped on a loose plank and fell, her ankle twisting painfully beneath her. As she struggled to stand, the mammoth closed in, its earth-shaking footsteps growing louder with each passing second. Just as the mammoth was about to trample her, Brian heroically tackled her out of harm's way, narrowly avoiding a gruesome fate.

But the danger was far from over as they headed towards the exit. The couple found themselves trapped in a dense thicket of trees designed to feel like a forest, the mammoth's rage growing with each passing moment. They climbed the largest one, hoping to put some space between themselves and the furious creature. The mammoth, however, had other plans.

It reared up on its hind legs and slammed its massive body into the tree, sending the trunk shuddering from the impact. Emily and Brian clung to the branches for dear life, their hearts pounding in their chests as the mammoth continued its relentless assault.

With each thunderous impact, the tree began to splinter, threatening to collapse under the mammoth's fury. Knowing that they couldn't stay in the tree any longer, Emily and Brian stealthily climbed down to the ground, wincing as the mammoth's terrible roars echoed through the night. Brian helped Emily along the way as they darted from tree to tree, desperately trying to put some distance between themselves and the relentless beast.

Through a combination of luck and sheer determination, they managed to evade the mammoth and make their way to the edge of the park which was marked by a 20 foot tall barb-wire fence. With the mammoth closing in, Brian knew he had to act quickly to save Emily. With all his strength, he hoisted her up and over the fence, her fingers just barely grasping the top, using her jacket to help ease the sting of the barbs as she began to climb over and down to safety.

As the mammoth bore down on Brian, he screamed for Emily to keep going, knowing that his sacrifice would ensure her survival. Her heart was breaking as she heard her boyfriend's desperate cries and there was nothing she could do.

With one final, gut-wrenching scream, Brian was silenced as the mammoth dragged him back into the park. Emily, devastated by her loss, could only watch in horror as the love of her life was swallowed by the darkness.

The horrifying tale of the night at La Brea Tar Pits would forever haunt Emily, a chilling reminder of the ancient evils that lay hidden beneath the earth. The memory of Brian's bravery and sacrifice would stay with her, a testament to the power of love in the face of unimaginable terror.

Terror in the Swamps

Dennis, a seasoned reptile trainer at an alligator farm in Florida, began his day like any other. He grabbed his bucket of fresh meat and headed out to the pit where the gators eagerly awaited their morning feast. However, as he approached the pit, he was shocked to find all the gators partially eaten, lying lifeless on the ground. Saddened and confused, Dennis noticed a gruesome trail of flesh and blood leading away from the pit.

Following the grisly path, he discovered a massive hole in the back fencing of the farm, leading straight into the swamps. With a sense of dread, he realized that whatever had caused this carnage was still out there, lurking in the murky waters.

Meanwhile, a family of four and their tour guide embarked on an airboat ride through the swamps, blissfully unaware of the horror that awaited them. The airboat glided smoothly over the water, the children's laughter filling the air as they marveled at the sights around them.

Suddenly, the airboat struck something massive beneath the water, sending the vessel and its passengers flying through the air. The two young boys, their parents, and the tour guide were thrown into the water, panic rising in their throats as they struggled to get back onto the boat.

The tour guide, sensing the urgency of the situation, helped each family member back onto the airboat. Just as he was assisting the mother back into the boat, something yanked him beneath the water's surface. He sacrificed himself to save her as moments later, his lifeless torso was flung onto the boat, sending the family into a state of abject terror.

The father desperately tried to start the airboat, but the engine refused to turn over. The water around them began to churn, and even the alligators on the shore fled in fear as the mysterious creature drew closer from under the water. The family huddled together, their hearts pounding as they braced themselves for the worst.

The creature finally revealed itself about 30 feet from the boat, its grotesque, mutated alligator-reptile hybrid face emerging from the depths. The sight of the monster filled the family with unimaginable horror, and as it leapt from the water, it seemed that all hope was lost.

Just then, Dennis roared onto the scene in his own airboat, charging straight at the creature. The tip of his boat struck the monster's head with a sickening crack, shattering its skull and killing it instantly. The creature sank lifelessly to the bottom of the swamp, where alligators from all around re-appeared and swarmed in to feast on the prehistoric carcass.

Dennis helped the terrified family onto his airboat, managing a weak smile as he quipped, "Anyone care for some new boots?" Carefully navigating the blood red waters they made their way back to safety, shaken but alive, their harrowing encounter with the last remaining giant alligator a story they would never forget.

The Expedition of Terror

Dr. Abigail Simmons, a renowned paleontologist, led a team of researchers on an expedition deep into the Amazon rainforest to search for an undiscovered dinosaur species. The team consisted of her trusted colleague Dr. James Peterson, their field assistant Laura, and a local guide named Diego.

One day, while exploring a remote riverbank, they stumbled upon an extraordinary find: a nest of large, seemingly fossilized eggs partially buried in the mud. Excitement surged through the team as they realized they were on the brink of a groundbreaking discovery.

As they carefully excavated the eggs, they noticed strange markings on nearby trees. Diego, familiar with the local legends, warned the group that they had disturbed the resting place of a cursed dinosaur species. However, his caution fell on deaf ears, as the researchers were too consumed with their discovery to pay heed to the local superstitions.

That night, as the team slept soundly in their camp, the ground began to tremble. One by one, the fossilized eggs began to crack open, releasing creatures that had been trapped in time. The cursed dinosaurs grew to adult size almost immediately, twisted, monstrous, and hungry for revenge on those who had disturbed their resting place.

The expedition team awoke to the sounds of snarls and roars, their hearts pounding in terror as they found themselves surrounded by the nightmarish creatures. The dinosaurs were unlike anything they had ever seen – a grotesque fusion of prehistoric species, part Tyrannosaurus and part stegosaurus with razor-sharp claws, rows of serrated teeth, hardened scales and

a thirst for blood. In a desperate attempt to slow the creatures
down, Dr. Simmons devised a plan. They would create a di-
version by setting fire to their camp, hoping the flames would
distract the dinosaurs long enough for them to find a way out
of the jungle with heavy hearts, the team set their research and
supplies ablaze, watching as the fire roared to life. The plan
worked, and the dinosaurs were drawn to the inferno, their
sinister eyes reflecting the dancing flames.

While the creatures were momentarily distracted, the team
made their escape, Diego, using his knowledge of the terrain,
led the group through the dense jungle, weaving in and out of
the trees to confuse their relentless pursuers.

As the team made their escape through the dense foliage, they
were all too aware of the hidden dangers that lurked around
every corner still. The rainforest was a treacherous place,
teeming with poisonous plants and venomous creatures, waiting for the opportunity to strike.

Catching their breath and taking a short break Dr. Simmons
felt something brush against her leg. Thinking it was just
another vine, she reached down to move it out of her way. As
she grasped the vine, she realized with horror that it was not a
plant, but a highly venomous snake: a bushmaster, known for
its aggressive behavior and deadly bite.

The snake, startled by the sudden contact, reared back, preparing to strike her. She found herself frozen, staring down the
snake's unblinking eyes, its forked tongue flicking in and out
menacingly.

In the split second before the snake lunged, Dr. Peterson
sprang into action. Using a long, sturdy branch, he swiftly
pinned the snake's head to the ground, preventing it from
striking Dr. Simmons.

The snake writhed and hissed, its fangs bared as it fought against the pressure of the branch. Diego walked over and with his machete made sure it wasn't going to bite anyone anymore...

Dr. Simmons, her heart still pounding, turned to Dr. Peterson and Diego and thanked them for their quick thinking and bravery. The incident had left them all shaken but more determined than ever to rely on each other to escape this nightmare.

Hours later the team reached the edge of the rainforest, they began to think they had finally escaped the cursed dinosaurs' relentless pursuit. They allowed themselves a moment of relief, their hearts still pounding with the adrenaline of their harrowing journey. But just as they thought they were safe, the chilling sounds of snarls and roars echoed through the trees, signaling that their nightmare was far from over.

The grotesque dinosaurs reappeared, bursting through the foliage with rage-filled eyes, intent on hunting down the intruders who had disturbed their slumber. The team's hope quickly turned to despair, as they realized they had been too naive to think they could outrun the ancient terrors.

In a last-ditch effort to save themselves, Diego recalled an old native technique for survival, passed down through generations. He quickly instructed the team to cover themselves in mud, masking their scent and blending into the environment. They smeared the mud on their skin and clothes, their hands shaking with fear and urgency.

Hidden in the shadows, the team watched as the dinosaurs stalked past them, searching for their prey. The creatures' breaths were hot and rancid, their enormous bodies casting ominous shadows on the ground. As they waited, the tension in the air was suffocating, the weight of the silence crushing them.

In a cruel twist of fate, Diego's mud-covered boot slipped on a wet rock, sending a resounding splash through the still air. The dinosaurs' attention was immediately drawn to the sound, their eyes narrowing in on the source.

The team watched in horror as Diego, their loyal guide, heroically drew the dinosaurs away from them, sacrificing himself for their survival. His screams and cries echoed through the rainforest, followed by the guttural roars of the monstrous predators.

With heavy hearts and immense gratitude for Diego's bravery, the team resumed their journey to safety, leaving the horrifying scene behind. The tragedy of Diego's sacrifice would forever haunt their memories, a grim reminder of the price they had paid for delving into the ancient secrets hidden deep within the Amazon rainforest.

As they returned to civilization, Dr. Simmons and Dr. Peterson vowed never to forget the terrible creatures they had awakened, Diego's sacrifice and the lesson they had learned: that some secrets were best left undiscovered.

THE END.

Chris Levine is an accomplished author and Hollywood actor known for igniting young imaginations with delightful dinosaur adventures. While he has previously crafted engaging dinosaur tales for early readers, Chris decided to take a walk on the wild side with Jurassic Terrors, a thrilling, spine-tingling adventure perfect for kids to share at sleepovers, reminiscent of the stories we cherished in our own childhoods. When not crafting captivating narratives, Mr. Levine can be found gracing both the stage and screen in the Los Angeles area. With a passion for paleontology and storytelling, he aspires to bring adults into a world of prehistoric wonder through an upcoming adult fiction dinosaur series.

Olesea Vladimir, a freelance illustrator and graphic designer, based in sunny Moldova. All she does is breathe life into diverse visual inspirations by art. But her heart has a special place for dinosaurs, these mesmerizing beings from a bygone era, remain an enduring source of fascination, as none of us ever had the privilege of witnessing them in the flesh. That's precisely why delving into the world of dinosaurs is an endlessly captivating adventure.

www.ingramcontent.com/pod-product-compliance
Lightning Source LLC
Chambersburg PA
CBHW070912160726
48004CB00003B/1341